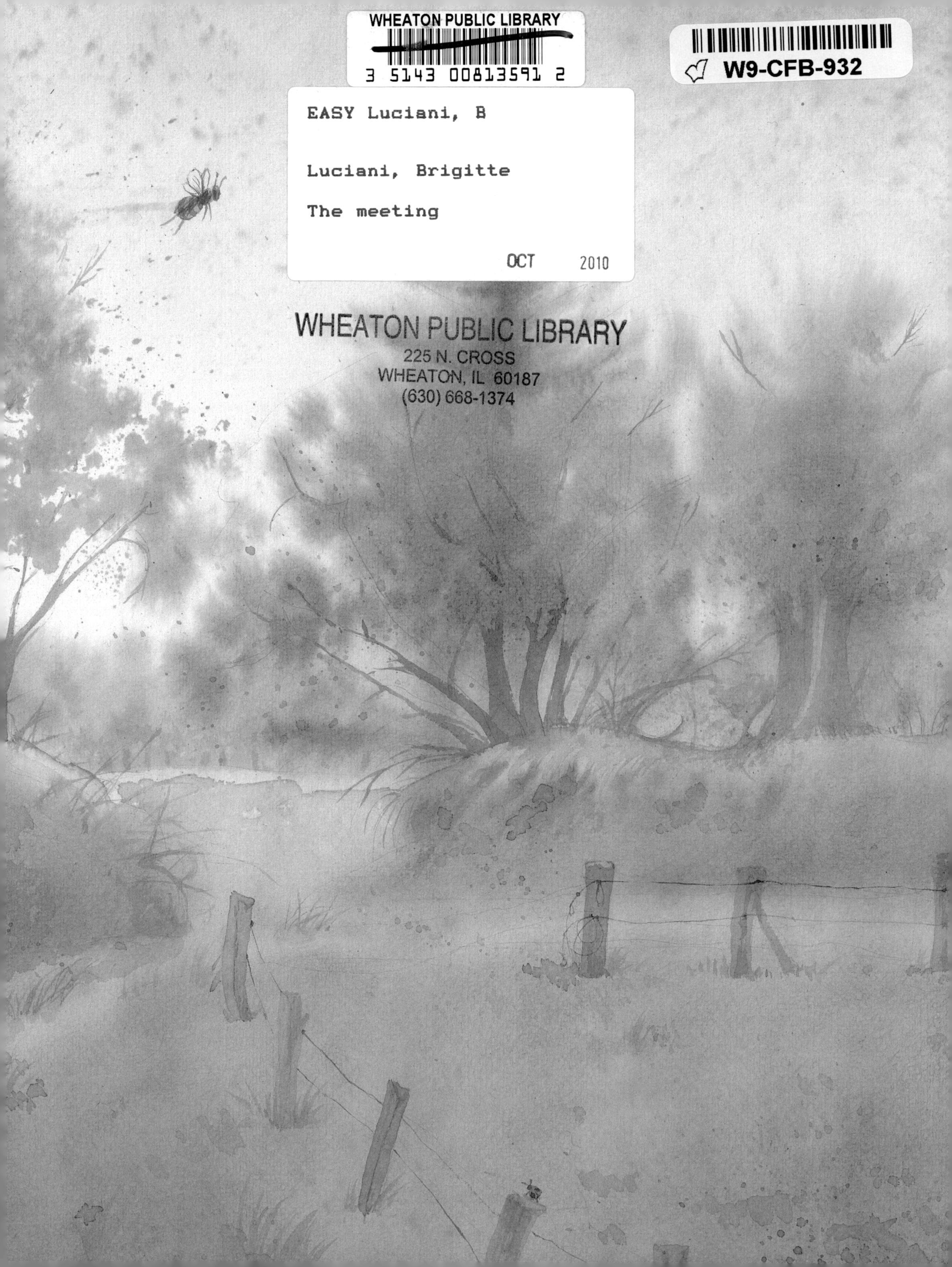

MR. BADGER AND MRS. FOX #1

THE MEETING

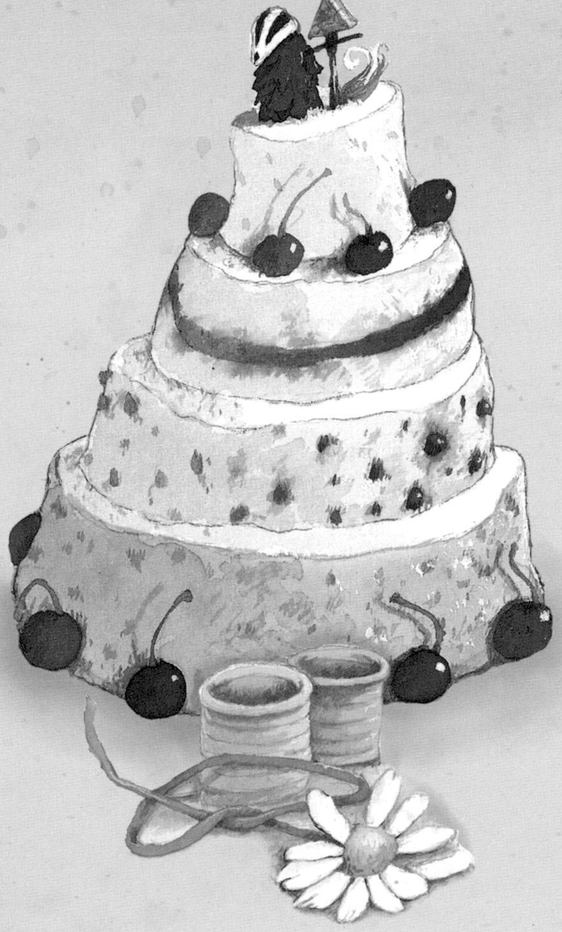

Brigitte LUCIANI & Eve THARLET

Graphic Universe™ • Minneapolis • New York

Thank you to Chris for the proofreading,
the support, and the patience.
—B.L.

Thank you to Nicole R., who agreed with
enthusiasm to check my scribbled drawings and
lettering along with the "li'l foxes" in her class.
—E.T.

Story by Brigitte Luciani
Art by Eve Tharlet
Translation by Carol Klio Burrell

First American edition published in 2010 by Graphic Universe™.
Published by arrangement with MEDIATOON LICENSING - France.

Monsieur Blaireau et Madame Renarde
1/La rencontre
© DARGAUD 2006 - Tharlet & Luciani
www.dargaud.com

English translation copyright © 2010 Lerner Publishing Group, Inc.

Graphic Universe™ is a trademark of Lerner Publishing Group, Inc.

Graphic Universe™
A division of Lerner Publishing Group, Inc.
241 First Avenue North
Minneapolis, MN 55401 U.S.A.

Website address: www.lernerbooks.com

Library of Congress Cataloging-in-Publication Data

Luciani, Brigitte.
The meeting / by Brigitte Luciani ; illustrated by Eve Tharlet.
p.   cm. — (Mr. Badger and Mrs. Fox)
Summary: Having lost their home, a fox and her daughter move in with a
badger and his three children, but when the youngsters throw a big party
hoping to prove that they are incompatible, their plan backfires.
ISBN 978-0-7613-5625-7 (lib. bdg. : alk. paper)
[1. Single-parent families—Fiction. 2. Brothers and sisters—Fiction. 3. Badgers—Fiction.
4. Foxes—Fiction. 5. Toleration—Fiction.] I. Tharlet, Eve, ill. II. Title.
PZ7.L9713Mee 2010
[E]—dc22   2009032617

Manufactured in the United States of America
1 - DP - 12/15/09

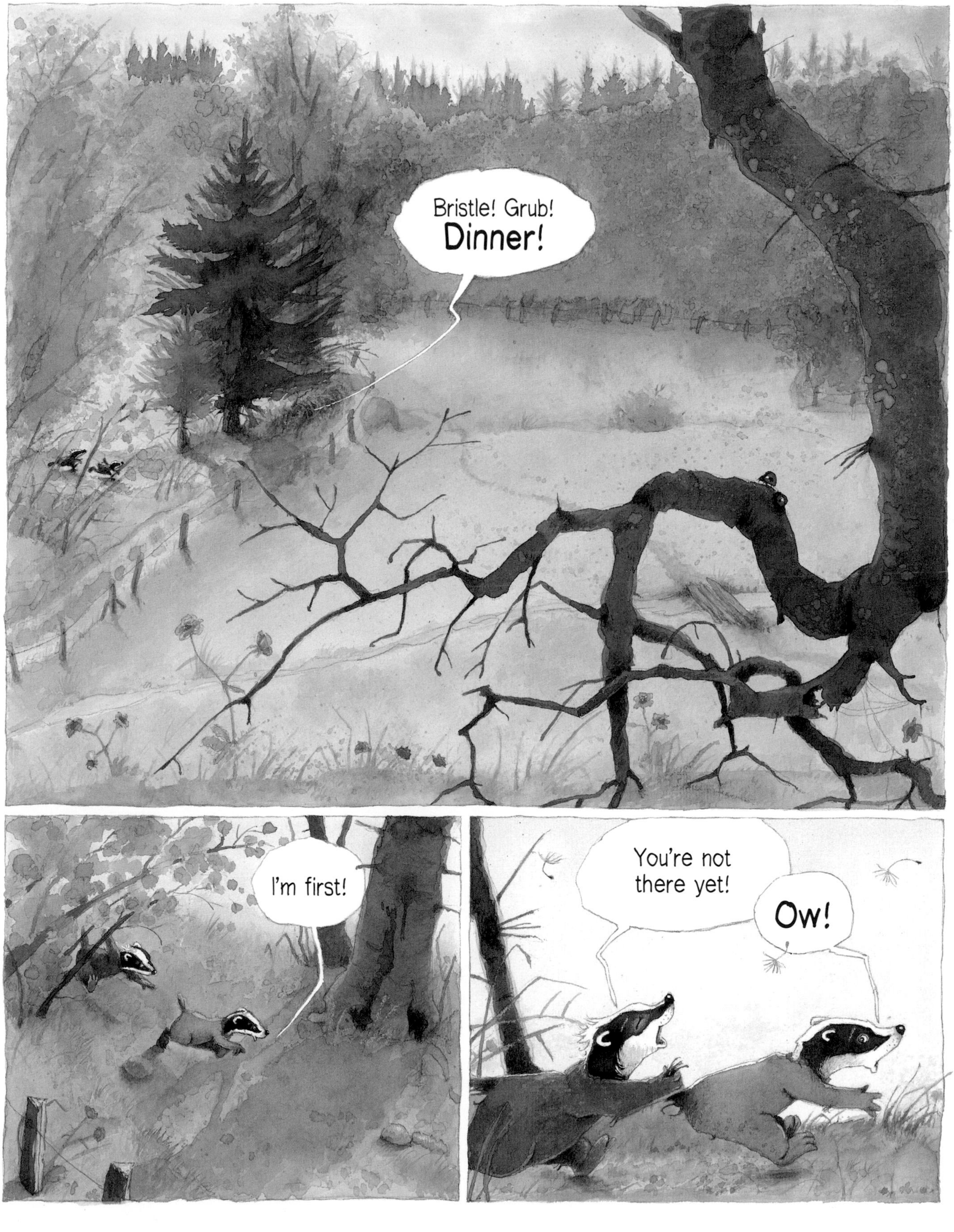
Bristle! Grub! Dinner!
I'm first!
You're not there yet!
Ow!

5912

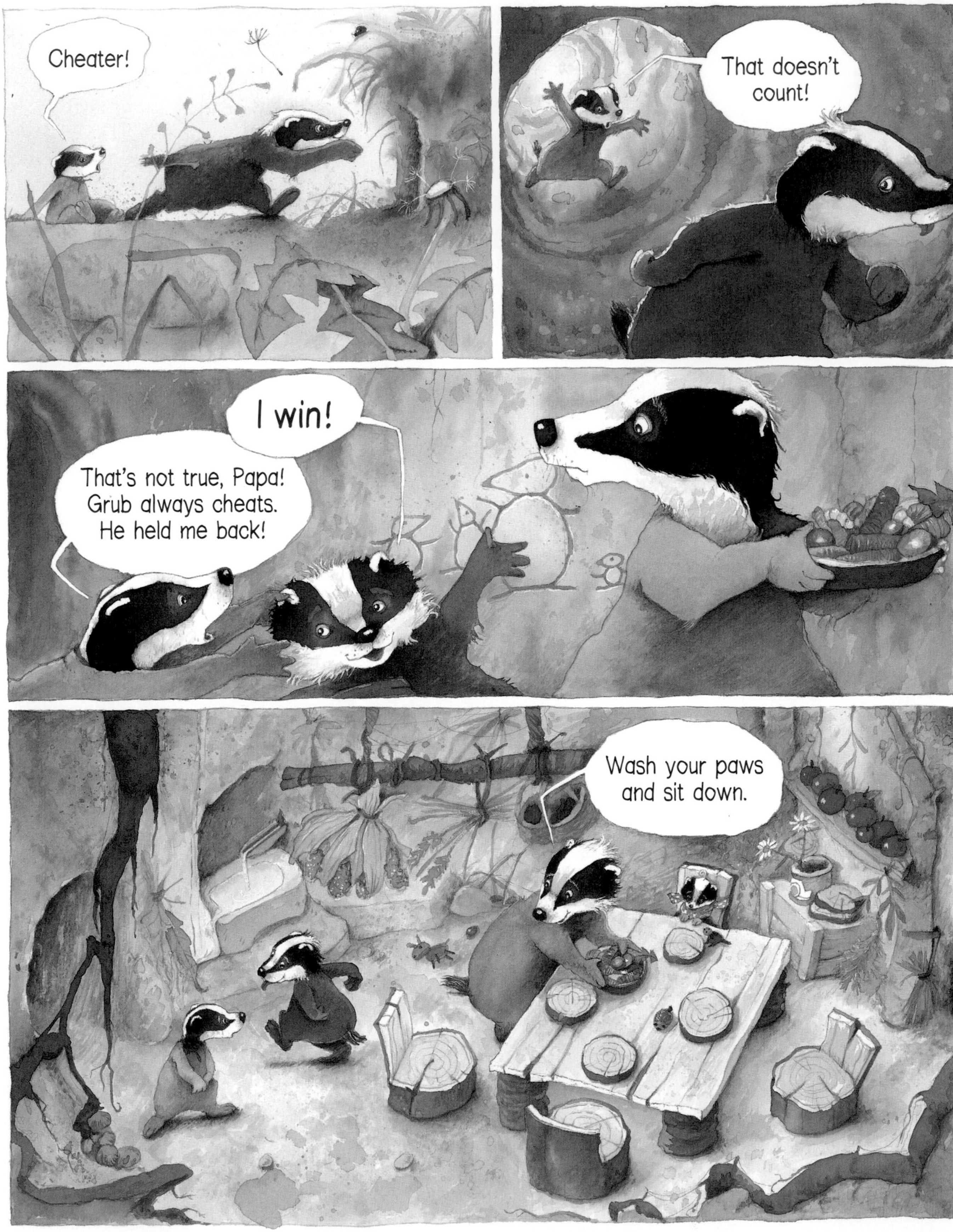
Cheater!
That doesn't count!
I win!
That's not true, Papa! Grub always cheats. He held me back!
Wash your paws and sit down.

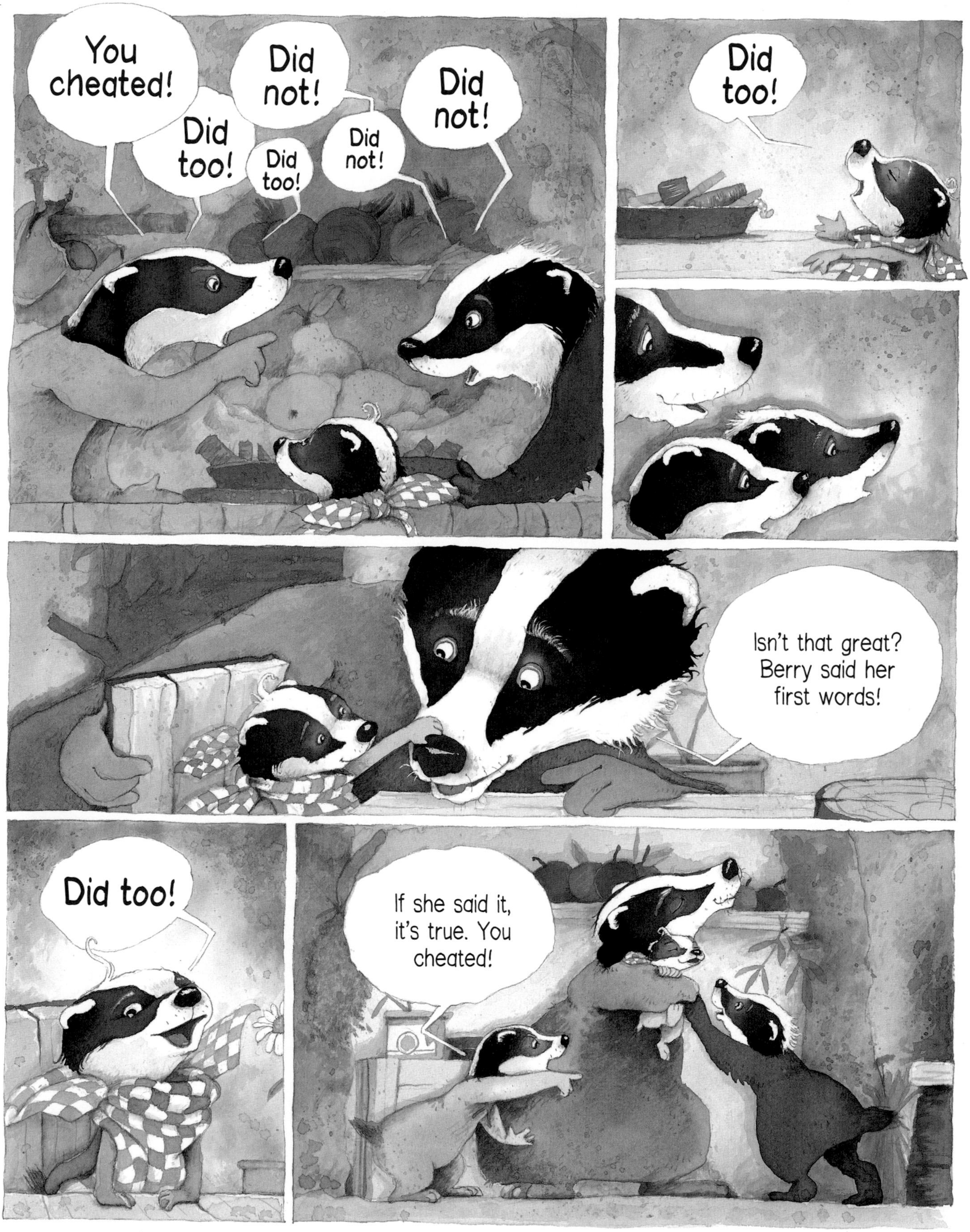
You cheated!
Did too!
Did not!
Did too!
Did not!
Did not!
Did too!
Isn't that great? Berry said her first words!
Did too!
If she said it, it's true. You cheated!

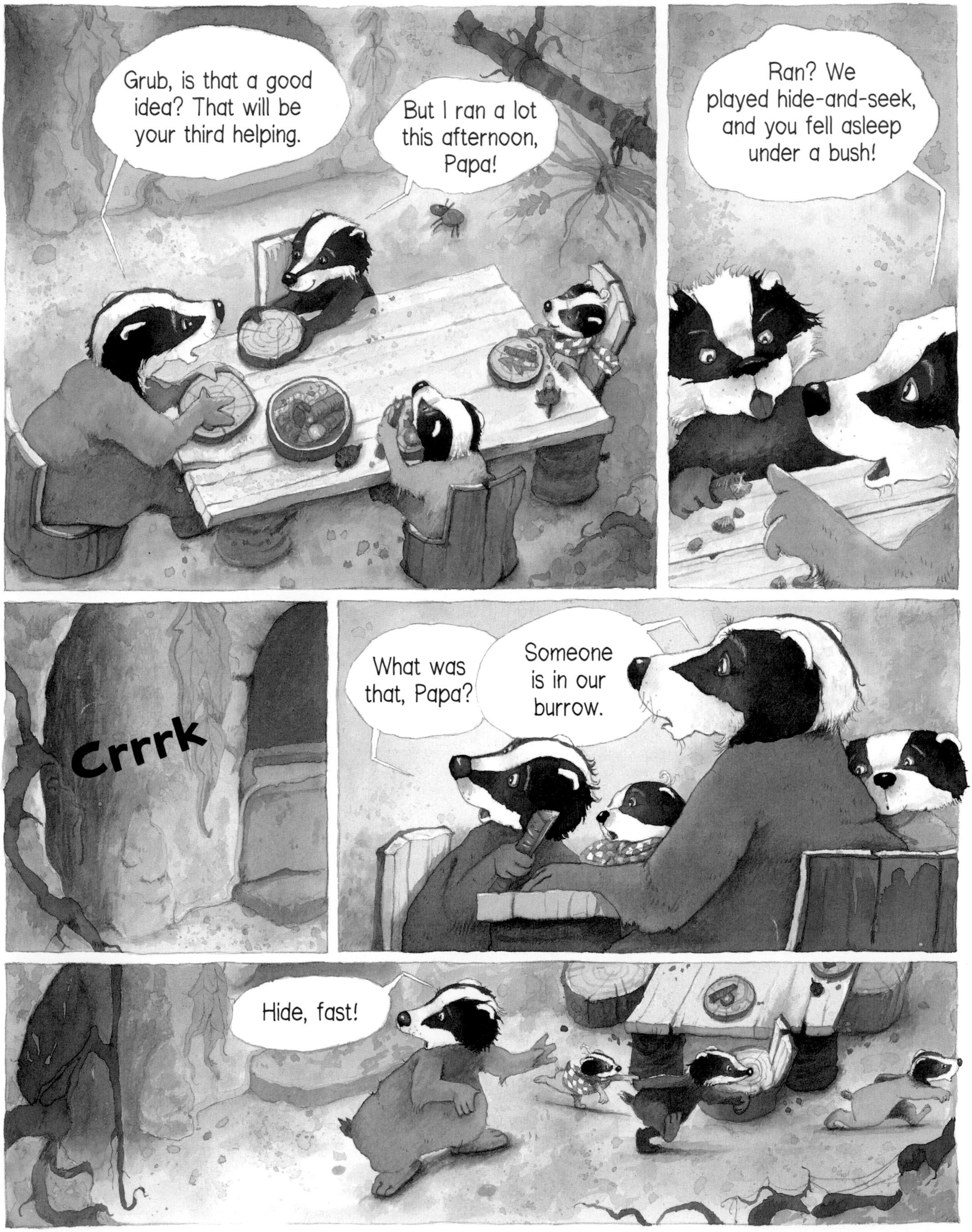
Grub, is that a good idea? That will be your third helping.
But I ran a lot this afternoon, Papa!
Ran? We played hide-and-seek, and you fell asleep under a bush!
Crrrk
What was that, Papa?
Someone is in our burrow.
Hide, fast!

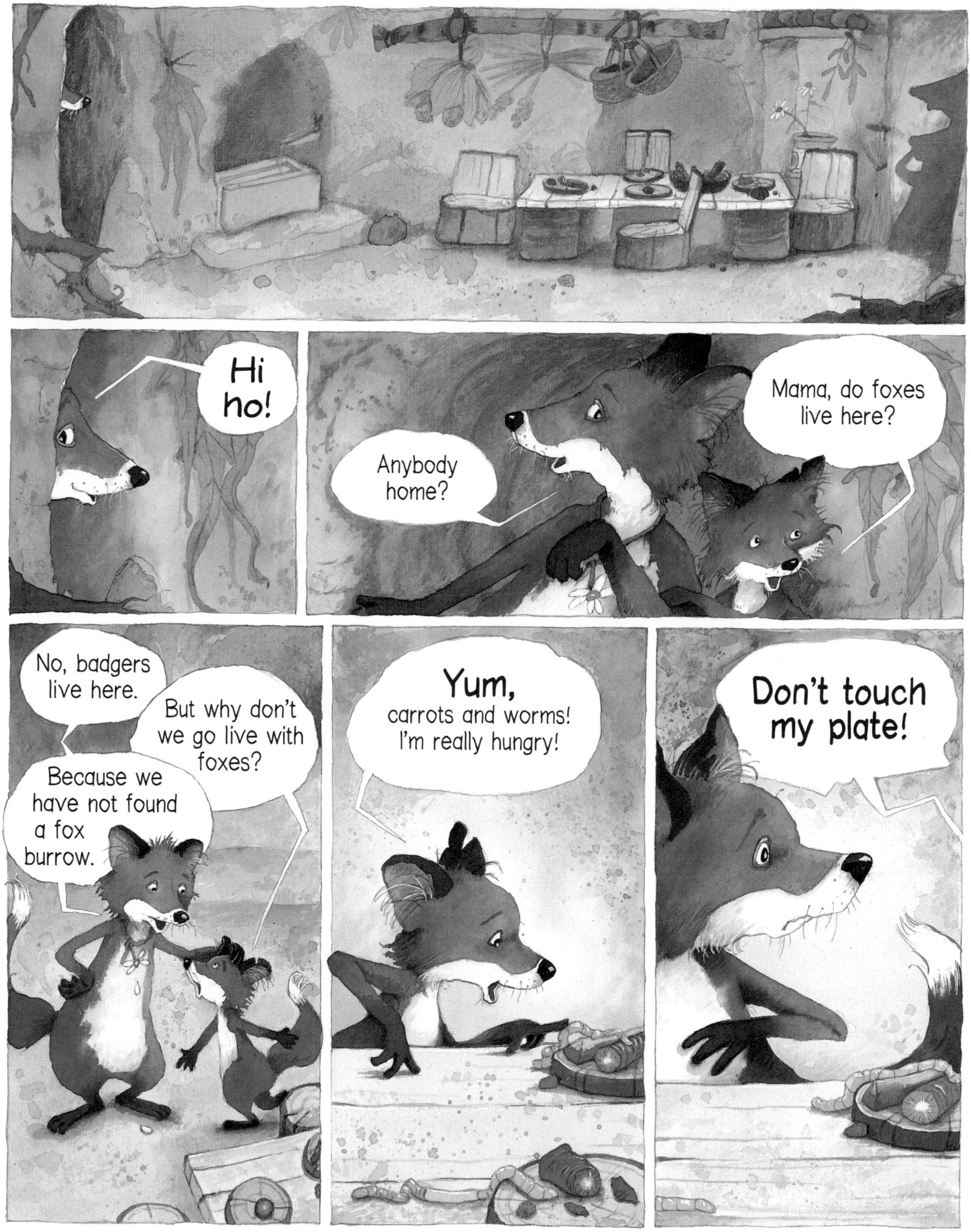
Hi ho!
Anybody home?
Mama, do foxes live here?
No, badgers live here.
But why don't we go live with foxes?
Because we have not found a fox burrow.
Yum, carrots and worms! I'm really hungry!
Don't touch my plate!

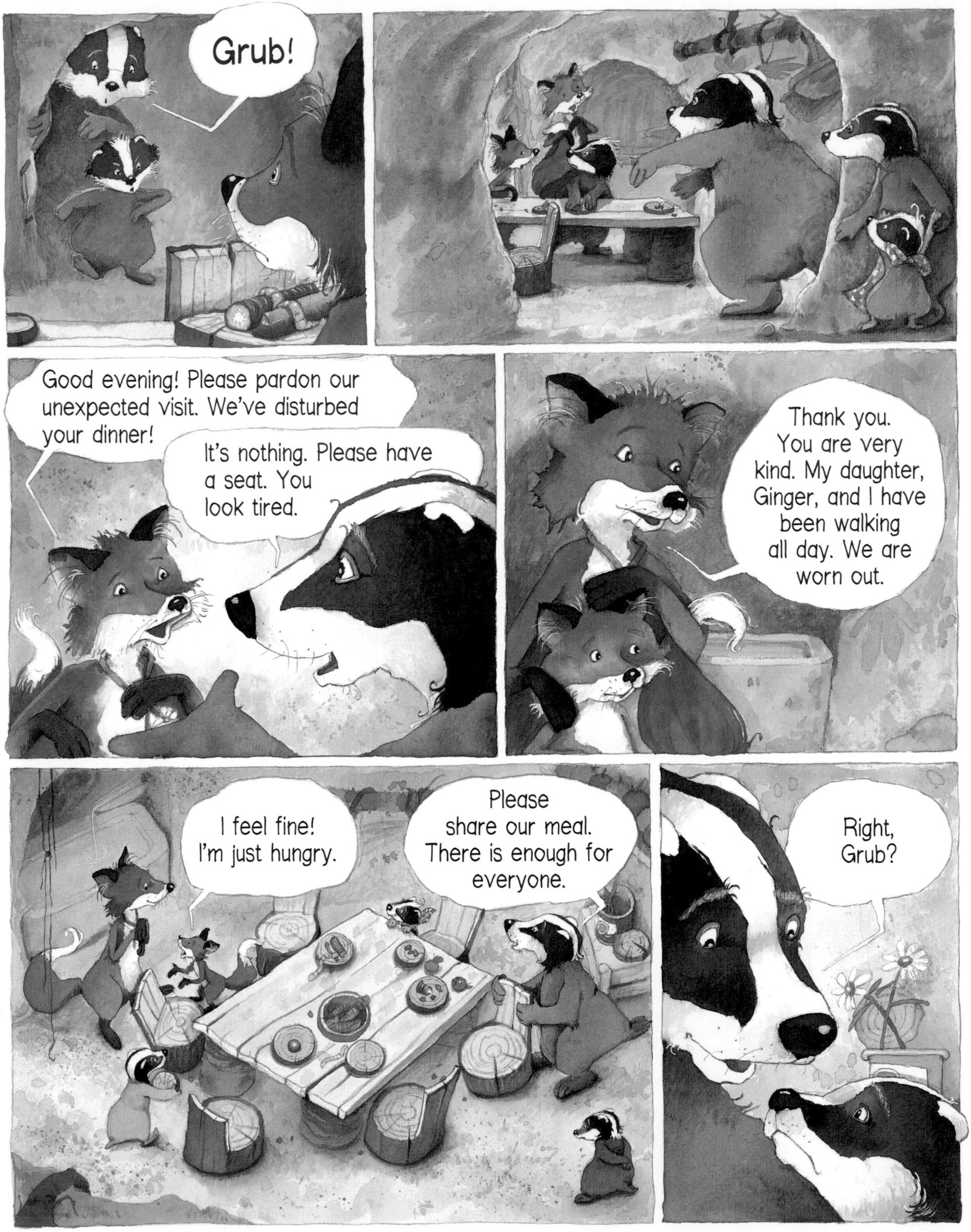
Grub!
Good evening! Please pardon our unexpected visit. We've disturbed your dinner!
It's nothing. Please have a seat. You look tired.
Thank you. You are very kind. My daughter, Ginger, and I have been walking all day. We are worn out.
I feel fine! I'm just hungry.
Please share our meal. There is enough for everyone.
Right, Grub?

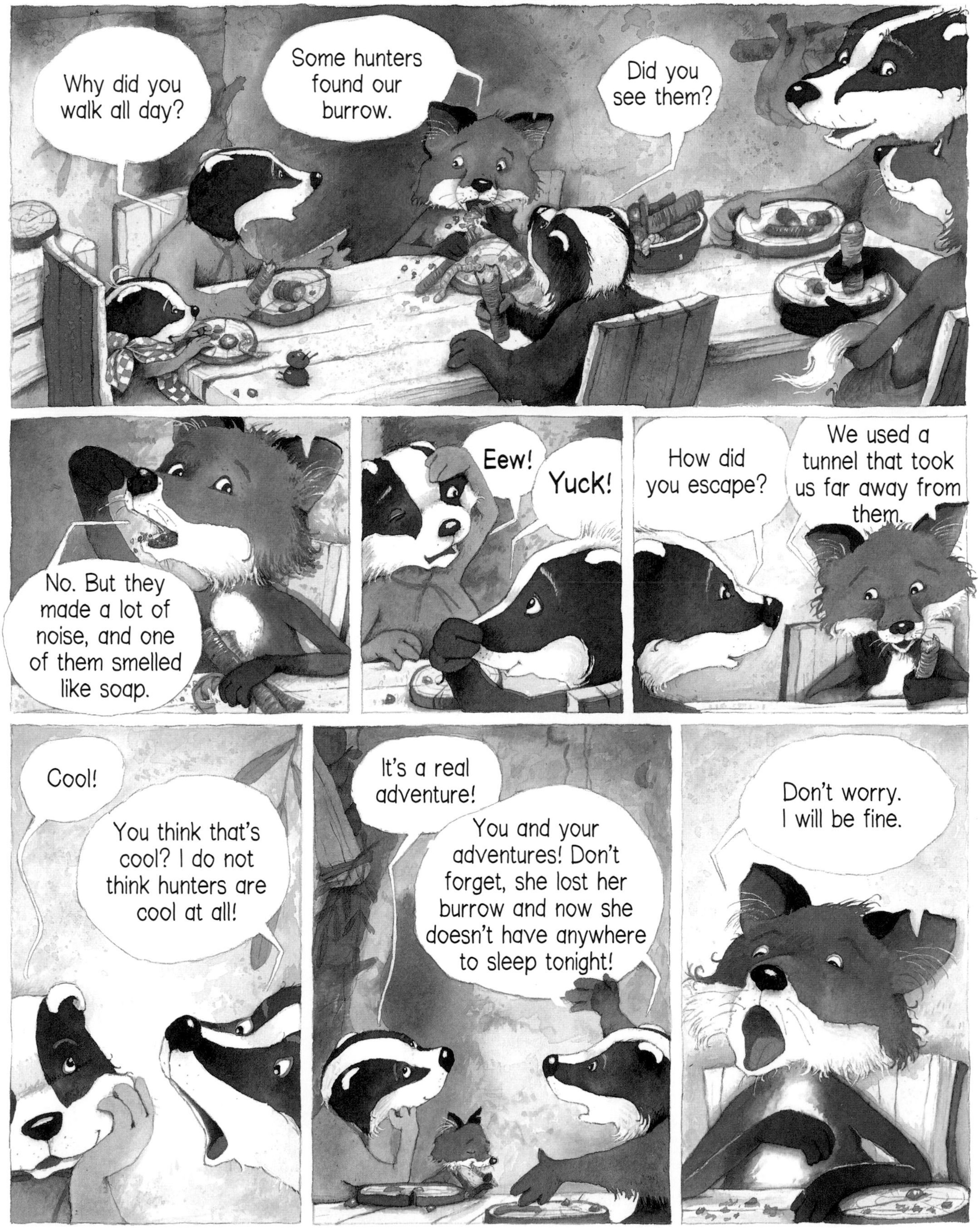
Why did you walk all day?
Some hunters found our burrow.
Did you see them?
No. But they made a lot of noise, and one of them smelled like soap.
Eew!
Yuck!
How did you escape?
We used a tunnel that took us far away from them.
Cool!
You think that's cool? I do not think hunters are cool at all!
It's a real adventure!
You and your adventures! Don't forget, she lost her burrow and now she doesn't have anywhere to sleep tonight!
Don't worry. I will be fine.

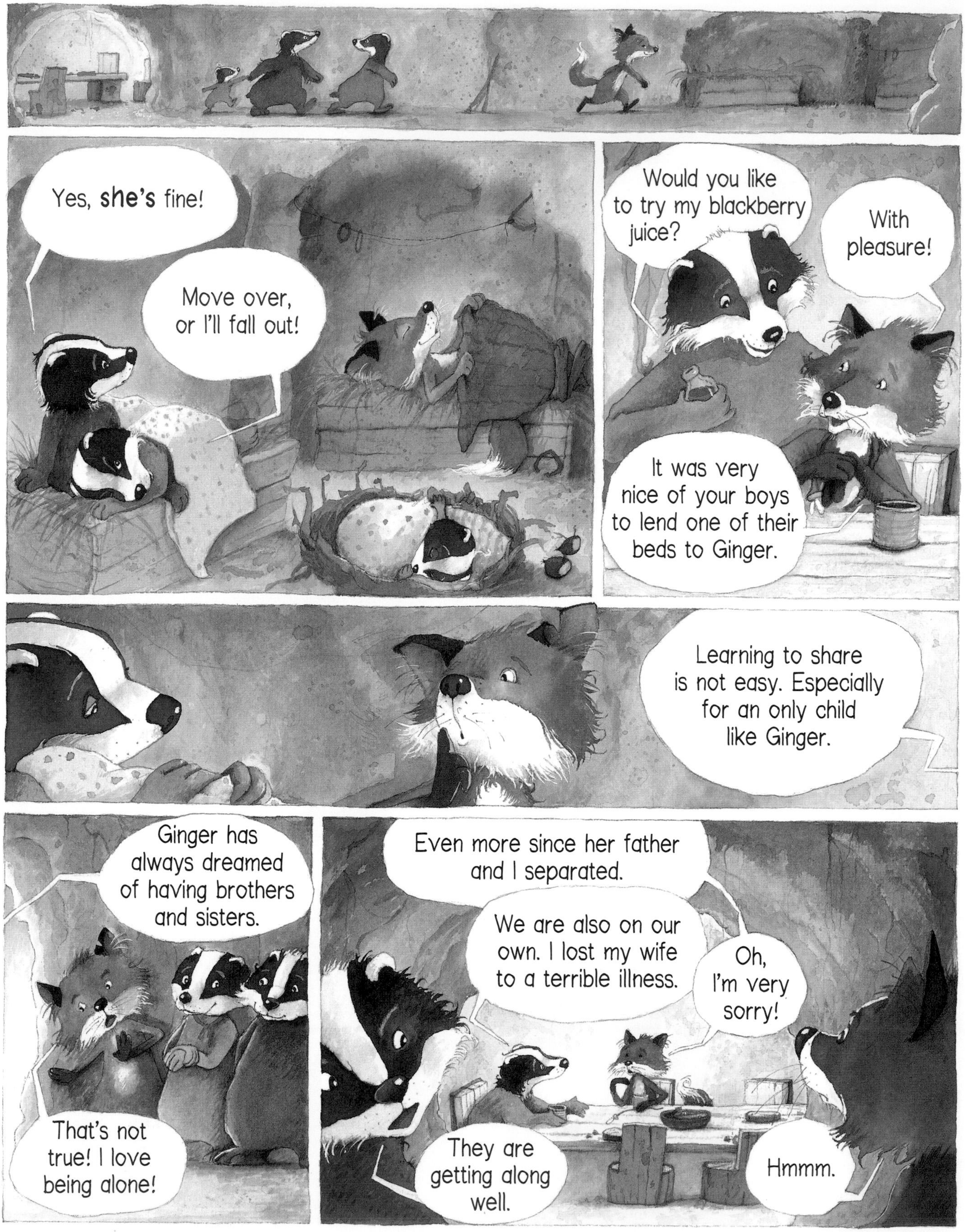
Yes, she's fine!
Move over, or I'll fall out!
Would you like to try my blackberry juice?
With pleasure!
It was very nice of your boys to lend one of their beds to Ginger.
Learning to share is not easy. Especially for an only child like Ginger.
Ginger has always dreamed of having brothers and sisters.
That's not true! I love being alone!
Even more since her father and I separated.
We are also on our own. I lost my wife to a terrible illness.
Oh, I'm very sorry!
They are getting along well.
Hmmm.

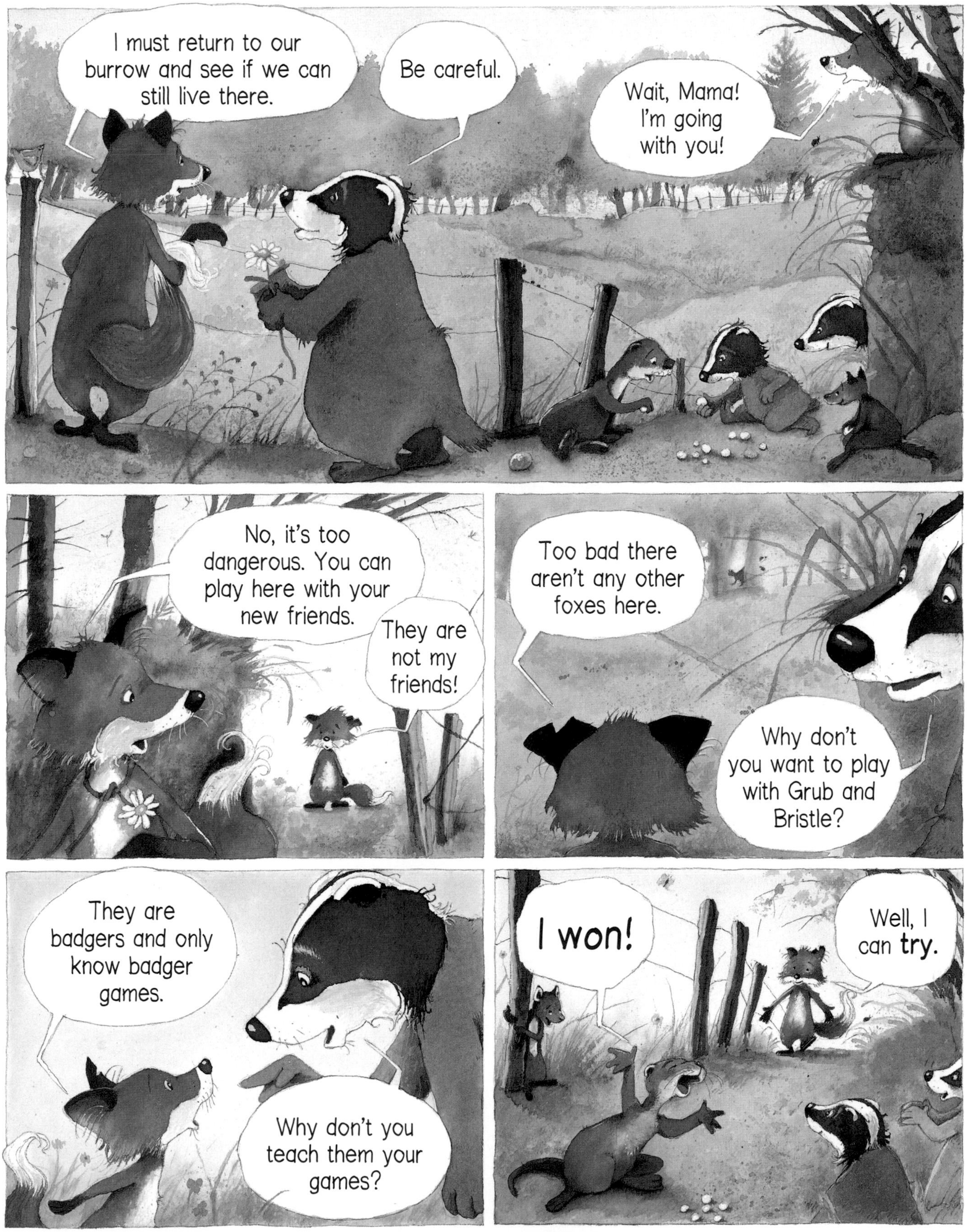
I must return to our burrow and see if we can still live there.
Be careful.
Wait, Mama! I'm going with you!
No, it's too dangerous. You can play here with your new friends.
They are not my friends!
Too bad there aren't any other foxes here.
Why don't you want to play with Grub and Bristle?
They are badgers and only know badger games.
Why don't you teach them your games?
I won!
Well, I can **try.**

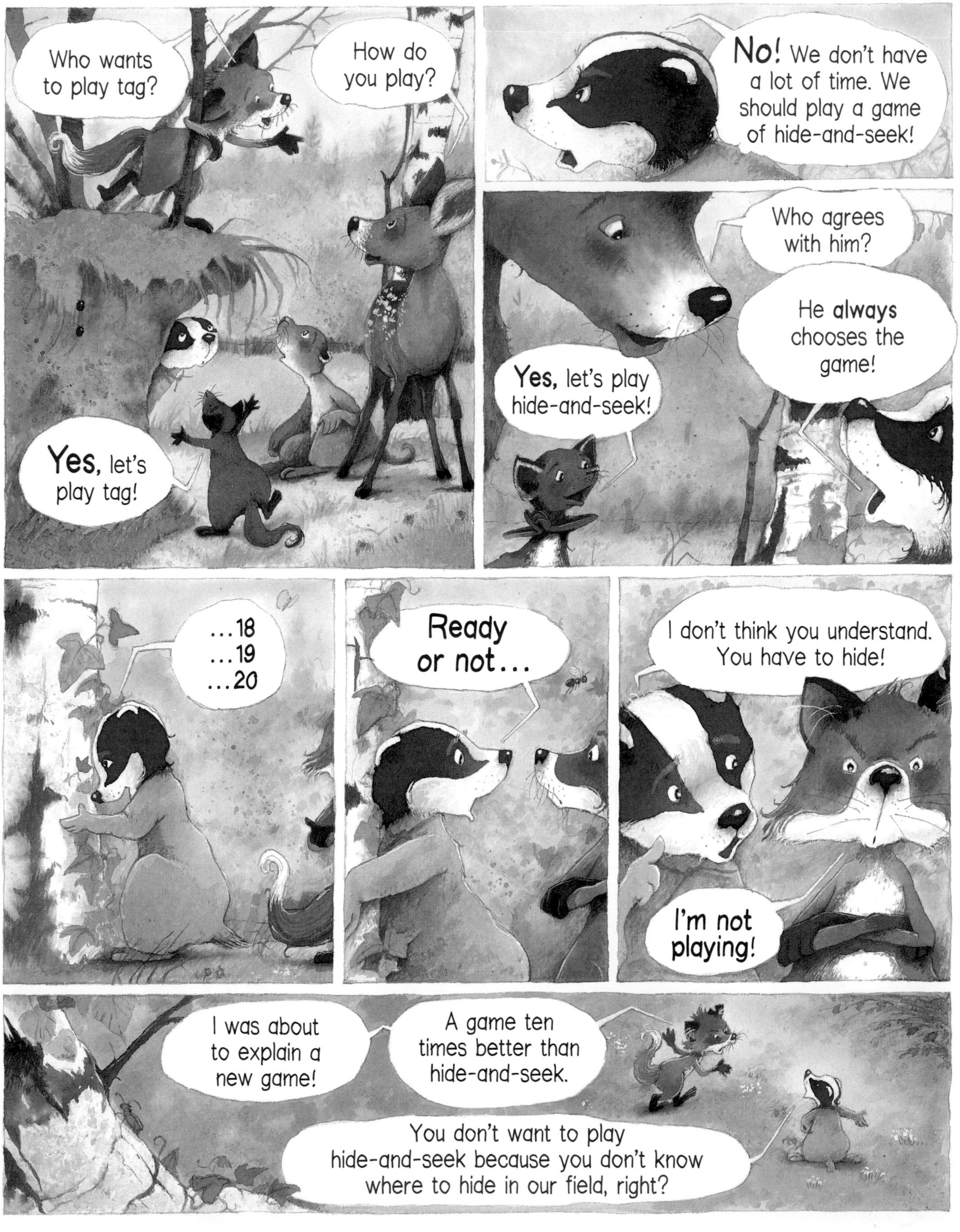
Who wants to play tag?
How do you play?
Yes, let's play tag!
No! We don't have a lot of time. We should play a game of hide-and-seek!
Who agrees with him?
He always chooses the game!
Yes, let's play hide-and-seek!
...18 ...19 ...20
Ready or not...
I don't think you understand. You have to hide!
I'm not playing!
I was about to explain a new game!
A game ten times better than hide-and-seek.
You don't want to play hide-and-seek because you don't know where to hide in our field, right?

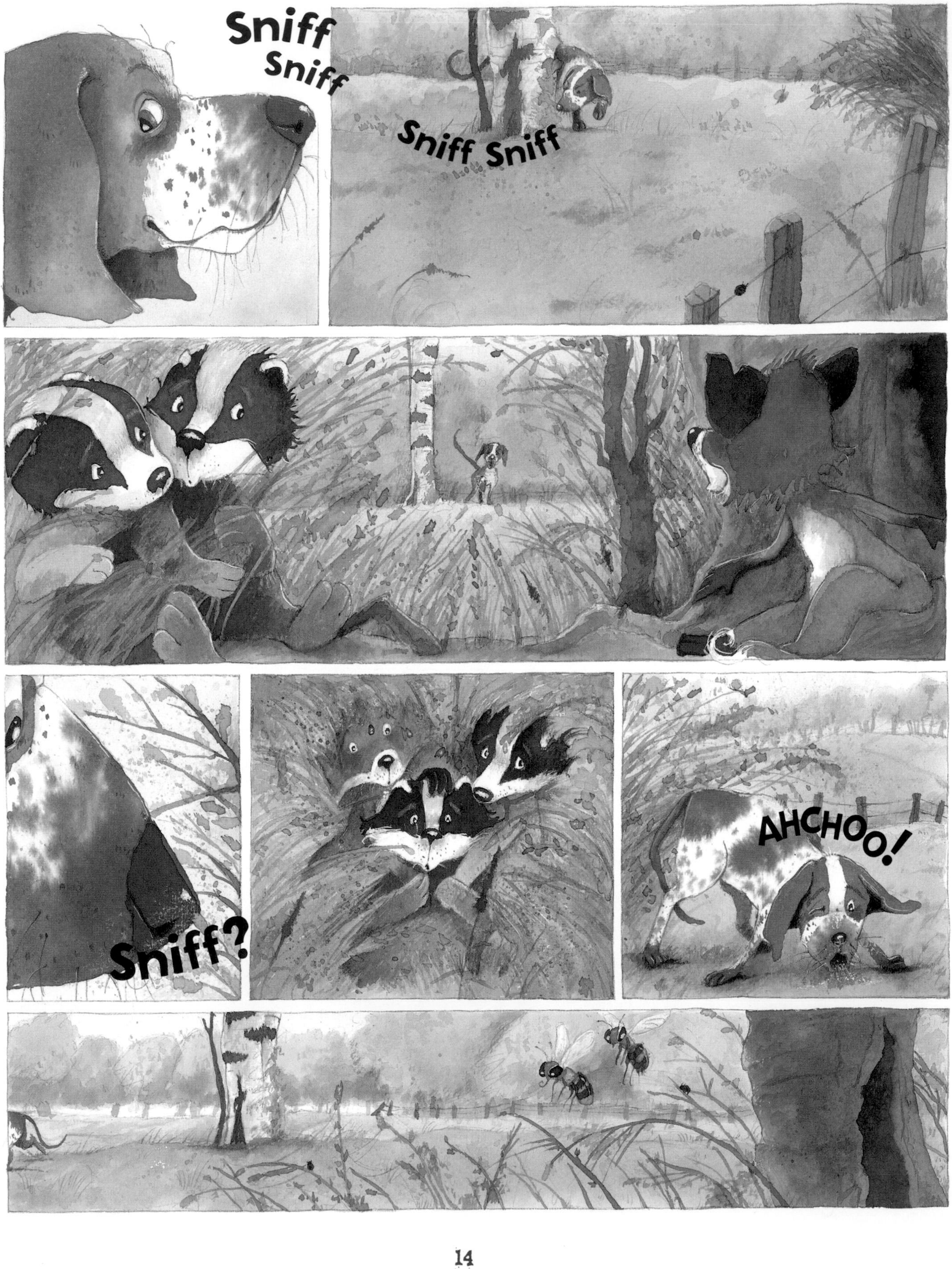
Sniff
Sniff
Sniff Sniff
Sniff?
AHCHOO!

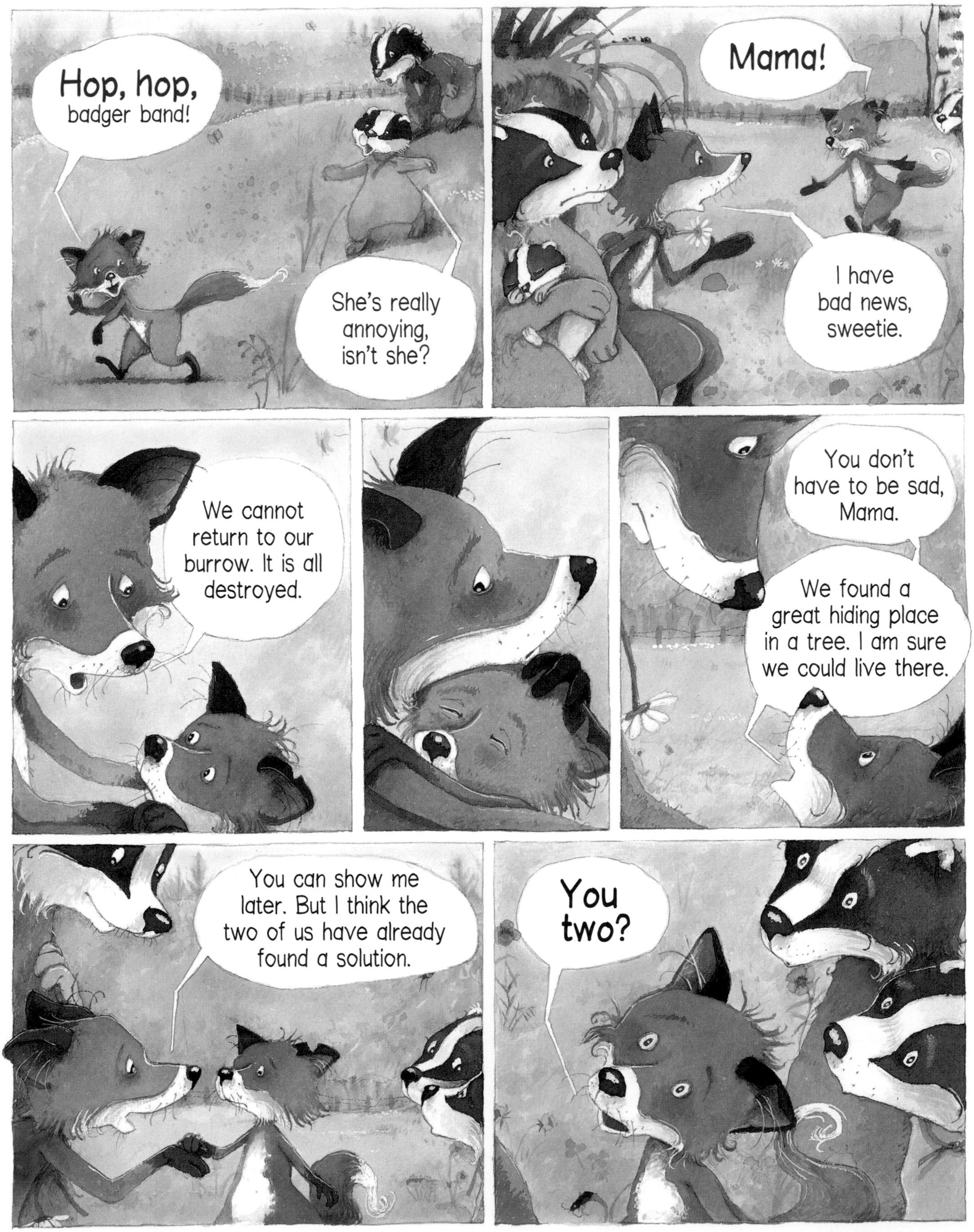
Hop, hop, badger band!
She's really annoying, isn't she?
Mama!
I have bad news, sweetie.
We cannot return to our burrow. It is all destroyed.
You don't have to be sad, Mama.
We found a great hiding place in a tree. I am sure we could live there.
You can show me later. But I think the two of us have already found a solution.
You two?

Edmund suggests we make his burrow larger so we can all live there.
I wanted to make the burrow larger anyway, so everyone can have his own room later.
In the meantime, the rooms can be for our guests.
It is an excellent solution until we find something else.
Now what's the problem?
Why can't we live in the tree?
I'll be happy when I finally get my bed back!
We're not the same type of animal and we should not live together!
There is nothing to discuss. That is how it will be. That's final.
Don't be afraid. We'll give it a try, and all will be well...
Grown-ups!
They ask you questions. Then, when you answer, they never want to listen.

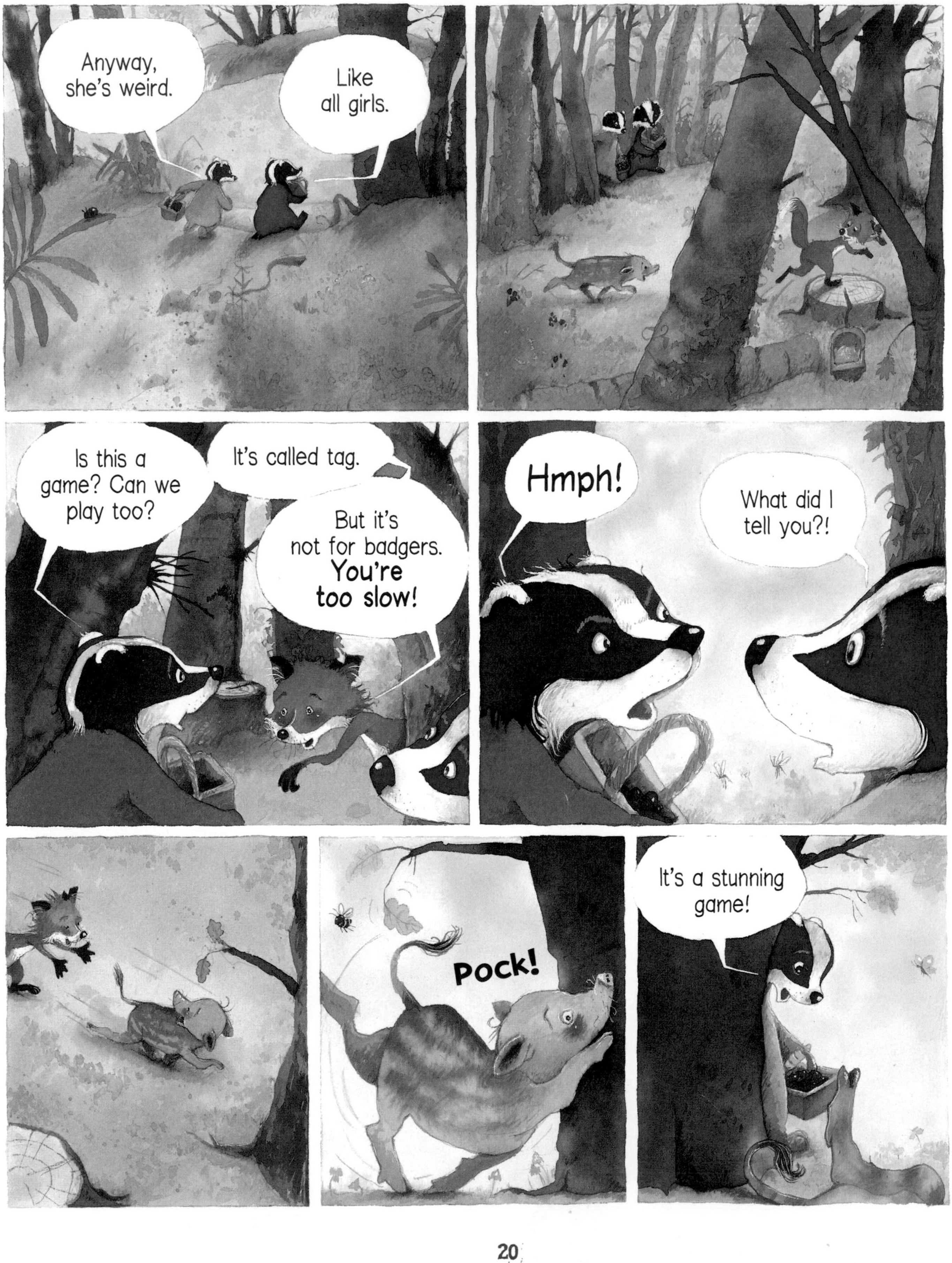
Anyway, she's weird.
Like all girls.
Is this a game? Can we play too?
It's called tag.
But it's not for badgers. You're too slow!
Hmph!
What did I tell you?!
Pock!
It's a stunning game!

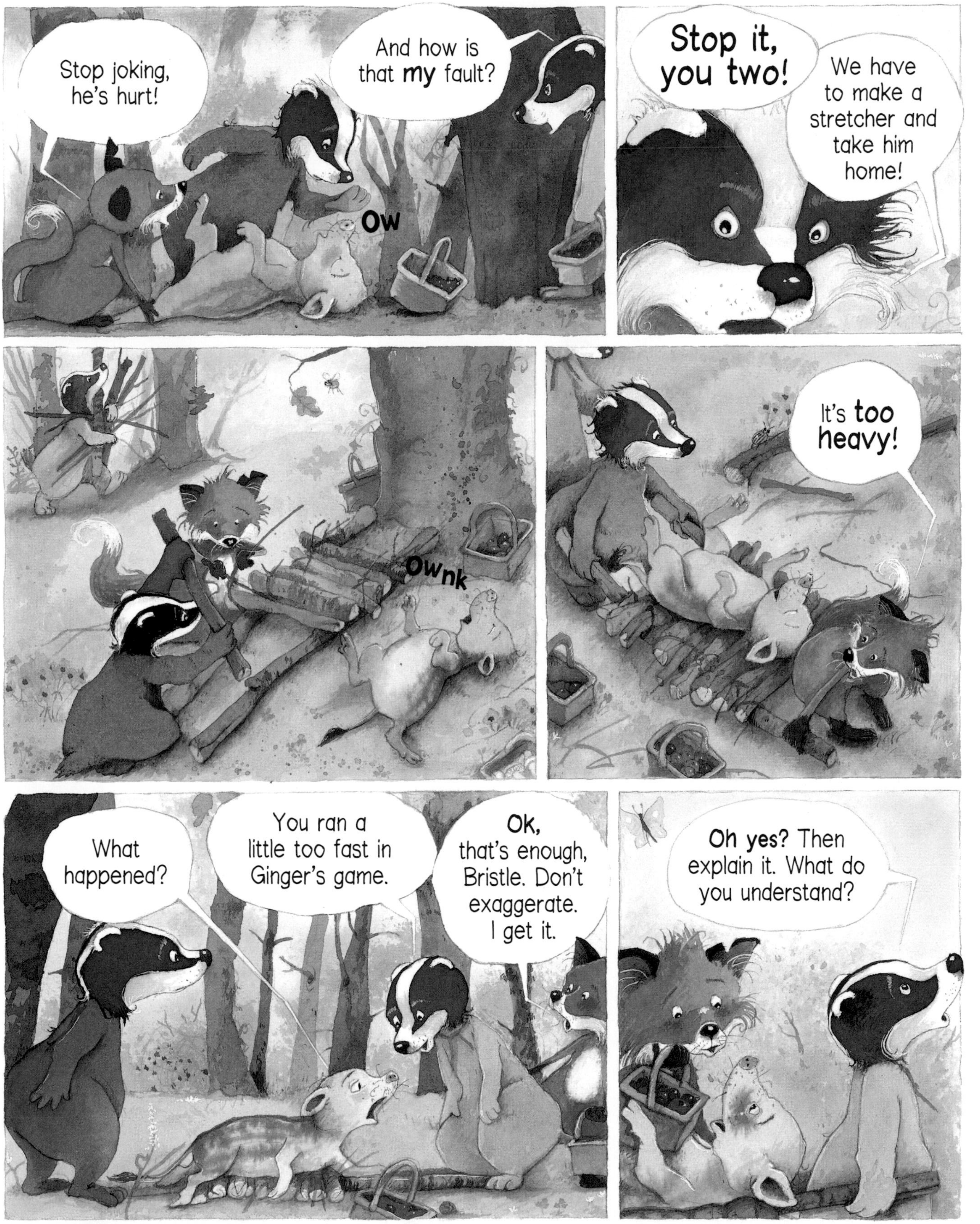
Stop joking, he's hurt!
And how is that **my** fault?
Ow
Stop it, you two!
We have to make a stretcher and take him home!
Ownk
It's **too heavy!**
What happened?
You ran a little too fast in Ginger's game.
Ok, that's enough, Bristle. Don't exaggerate. I get it.
Oh yes? Then explain it. What do you understand?

23

26

31

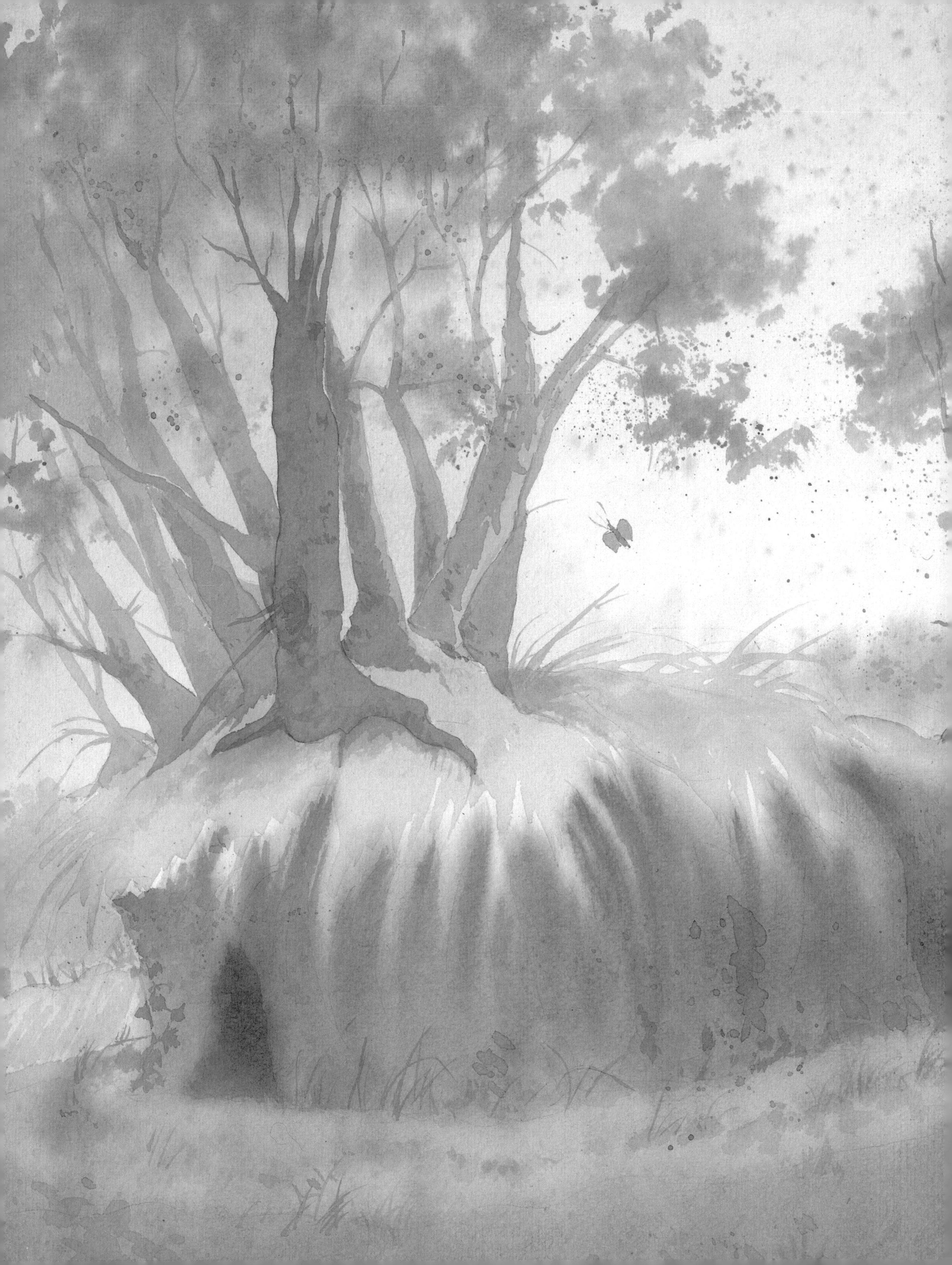